8.95

12

D1329618

jE
P

HATTIE
THE GOAT

Nettlepatch Farm

HATTIE THE GOAT

Abigail Pizer

Carolrhoda Books, Inc.
Minneapolis

This edition first published 1989 by Carolrhoda Books, Inc.

Original edition copyright © 1988 by Abigail Pizer.
Original edition published 1988 by Macmillan Children's Books, a division of
Macmillan Publishers Limited, London and Basingstoke.

Library of Congress Cataloging-in-Publication Data

Pizer, Abigail.
    Hattie the goat / by Abigail Pizer.
        p.   cm. — (Nettlepatch farm)
    Summary: A young goat enjoys eating everything on the farm, from
Mrs. Potter's vegetables to Mr. Potter's trousers.
    ISBN 0-87614-364-8 (lib. bdg.)
    1. Goats—Juvenile fiction. [1. Goats—Fiction. 2. Farm life—
Fiction.] I. Title. II. Series: Pizer, Abigail. Nettlepatch farm.
PZ10.3.P419Hat   1989   88-38284
[E]—dc19   CIP
                                                        AC

Manufactured in the United States of America

1 2 3 4 5 6 7 8 9 10 99 98 97 96 95 94 93 92 91 90 89

It is summertime at Nettlepatch Farm.
On the farm live Mr. Potter, Mrs. Potter,
and their little daughter, Amy.

All the farm animals are outside
in the sunshine.
The ducks are swimming in the pond.

The pigs and cows are grazing in
the fields.
Billingsgate is curled up comfortably on
the wall.

Hattie the goat is also enjoying
the sunshine.
She is nearly one year old, and this is
her very first summer.
The days are long, and she spends
them doing what she likes best: eating!

She likes eating grass,

she likes eating nettles,

and she likes eating blueberries—even the stalks!

Hattie will eat almost anything.

One morning, when Hattie is in the farmyard, she sees Mrs. Potter working in the vegetable garden. Then Hattie sees the vegetables—rows and rows of them.

The telephone is ringing in the farmhouse.
Mrs. Potter hurries inside.

Hattie looks at the gate. She looks at the farmhouse. Then she looks at the vegetables. In a moment she is through the gate.

She nibbles at the lettuce. She tries the beans.

She tastes the sweet peas.

But then Mrs. Potter comes back.
"What have you done, you greedy goat?"
Mrs. Potter chases Hattie out of
the garden.
Hattie knows she's been naughty.

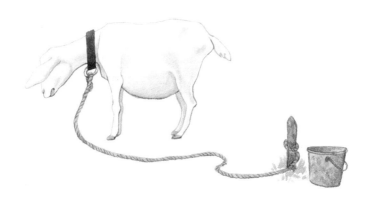

So Hattie is tied to a post by a rope. Although it is quite a long rope, Hattie does not like it. And she is still hungry. She tries chewing it. She goes on chewing it and chewing it, until...

She trots right back to the gate that leads
to the vegetable garden.
It is shut.
Then she sees a line of wash by the house.

She nibbles at some jeans. She tries a
T-shirt. She tastes some socks. They are

almost as good as the vegetables she ate.
Hattie enjoys Mr. Potter's trousers!

Just as she starts on one of Mr. Potter's shirts, she hears a shout. Mrs. Potter has seen her.
This time Hattie is tied to a stake by a metal chain.

She tries to chew the chain. That's no good. She tries pulling at the chain. She pulls hard. Has the stake moved a little?
She pulls and pulls and pulls, until...

...out comes the stake.

She is walking past the big barn when she notices that its doors are open.
Hattie has never been inside the barn. She puts her head around the door for a look.

Inside the barn are bales and bales of hay—more hay than Hattie has ever seen in her life.

Clink, clank goes the bucket as Hattie climbs up onto the mountain of hay.

Hattie eats and eats. Clink, clank goes the bucket; nibble, nibble goes Hattie. She eats so much she is quite uncomfortable. She can hardly stand up! Then Mr. Potter comes into the barn.

Mr. Potter is cross.
But he can see that Hattie has eaten more than
is good for her.
Hattie feels very sorry for herself.

Hattie is so full, she can't walk. Mr. Potter picks her up and carries her back to the farmyard.

This time Hattie doesn't need to be tied up. She feels so sick, she stays put. Hattie decides she will never eat again. Well, at least not until tomorrow.

Nettlepatch Farm

About the Author

Abigail Pizer studied at the Harrow School of Art in Harrow, England, and has a degree in illustration. Since leaving college in 1982, she has worked as a freelance illustrator. In addition to the Nettlepatch Farm books, she is the author and illustrator of *Harry's Night Out* and *Nosey Gilbert*. As a great animal lover, she writes most of her books about animals.